MW01180790

THE LIFE CYCLE OF A

Penguin

By Colleen Sexton

BELLWETHER MEDIA · MINNEAPOLIS, MN

Note to Librarians, Teachers, and Parents:

Blastoff! Readers are carefully developed by literacy experts and combine standards-based content with developmentally appropriate text.

Level 1 provides the most support through repetition of high-frequency words, light text, predictable sentence patterns, and strong visual support.

Level 2 offers early readers a bit more challenge through varied simple sentences, increased text load, and less repetition of high-frequency words.

Level 3 advances early-fluent readers toward fluency through increased text and concept load, less reliance on visuals, longer sentences, and more literary language.

Level 4 builds reading stamina by providing more text per page, increased use of punctuation, greater variation in sentence patterns, and increasingly challenging vocabulary.

Level 5 encourages children to move from "learning to read" to "reading to learn" by providing even more text, varied writing styles, and less familiar topics.

Whichever book is right for your reader, Blastoff! Readers are the perfect books to build confidence and encourage a love of reading that will last a lifetime!

This edition first published in 2010 by Bellwether Media, Inc.

No part of this publication may be reproduced in whole or in part without written permission of the publisher. For information regarding permission, write to Bellwether Media, Inc., Attention: Permissions Department, 5357 Penn Avenue South, Minneapolis, MN 55419.

Library of Congress Cataloging-in-Publication Data
Sexton, Colleen A., 1967–
  The life cycle of a penguin / by Colleen Sexton.
     p. cm. — (Blastoff! Readers life cycles)
  Includes bibliographical references and index.
  Summary: "Developed by literacy experts for students in kindergarten through grade three, this book follows penguins as they transform from eggs to adults. Through leveled text and related images, young readers will watch these creatures grow through every stage of life"—Provided by publisher.
  ISBN 978-1-60014-310-6 (hardcover : alk. paper)
  1. Penguins–Life cycles–Juvenile literature. I. Title.
  QL696.S473S49 2010
  598.4'4–dc22
                              2009037342

Printed in the United States of America, North Mankato, MN.
010110   1149

Contents

Penguins are **birds**. They do not fly.
They swim in the sea and walk on land.

There are 17 kinds of penguins. They all live in the southern half of the world. These **emperor penguins** live in icy **Antarctica**.

Penguins grow in stages. The stages of a penguin's **life cycle** are egg, chick, and adult.

adult

egg

chick

Adult emperor penguins leave the sea and make a long trip across the ice. They go to the same place every year to **breed**.

A male penguin **courts** a female.
They become **mates** for life.

The female penguin lays an egg after one month. The male uses his beak to scoop the egg onto his **webbed feet**.

The male tucks the egg under his **brood patch**. The egg stays warm under this flap of skin.

The female travels back to the sea to hunt for food.

The male penguin **huddles** with other males in the cold wind. His job for the next two months is to keep the egg safe and warm.

A chick grows inside the egg until it is ready to hatch. The chick pecks at the shell to crack it open.

Soft **down** feathers cover the new chick. The chick stays under its father's brood patch.

The female penguin returns. She brings up food from her stomach to feed her hungry chick.

The male penguin goes to the sea to hunt. He has not eaten for weeks.

The female tucks the chick under her brood patch. The chick eats and grows quickly.

Soon the chick is too big for the brood patch. It stays with other chicks while both its parents hunt for food.

The chick **molts**. Its down feathers fall out and waterproof feathers grow in.

The chick is eight months old. It has become a young adult. It can now swim in the sea and catch its own food.

In five years the penguin will find its own mate. Their egg will be the start of a new life cycle!

Glossary

Antarctica—the frozen continent that surrounds the south pole

bird—an animal with two legs, two wings, feathers, and a beak; penguins use their wings for swimming in the water instead of flying in the air.

breed—to join together to produce young

brood patch—a flap of skin on a bird that can cover an egg and keep it warm

court—to try to win over a mate; penguins make trumpeting sounds and bob their heads when they court.

down—small, soft feathers

emperor penguin—the largest kind of penguin; emperor penguins live in Antarctica.

huddle—to crowd together in a group

life cycle—the stages of life of an animal; a life cycle includes being born, growing up, having young, and dying.

mates—a male and female pair of animals

molt—to shed feathers so that new feathers can grow

webbed feet—feet that have toes connected by thin, flat skin; webbed feet help penguins swim quickly in water.

To Learn More

AT THE LIBRARY

Squire, Ann O. *Penguins.* New York, N.Y.: Children's Press, 2007.

Tate, Suzanne. *Perry Penguin: A Tale of a Brave Family.* Manteo, N.C.: Nags Head Art, Inc., 2007.

Wendorff, Anne. *Penguins.* Minneapolis, Minn: Bellwether Media, 2009.

ON THE WEB
Learning more about life cycles is as easy as 1, 2, 3.

1. Go to www.factsurfer.com.

2. Enter "life cycles" into the search box.

3. Click the "Surf" button and you will see a list of related Web sites.

With factsurfer.com, finding more information is just a click away.

Index

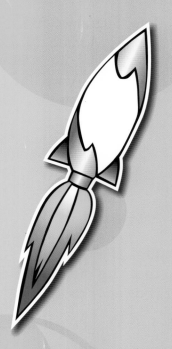

The images in this book are reproduced through the courtesy of: Frank Krahmer, front cover (adult), pp. 5, 6 (adult), 7; Sunset, front cover (egg), pp. 6 (egg), 9, 10; Frank Lukasseck, front cover (chick), pp. 6 (chick), 18; Juniors Bildarchiv, front cover (young chick), p. 13; Jan Vermeer, pp. 4, 21; All Canada Photos, p. 8; Alaska Stock Images, p. 11; Norbert Wu, p. 12; Joseph Van Os, p. 14; age fotostock, p. 15; Cill Curtsinger, p. 16; Keren Su, pp. 17, 20; Sue Flood, p. 19.